The Weeds & the Weather

By
MARY STOLZ

Pictures by
N. CAMERON WATSON

 Greenwillow Books, New York

Thanks to two handsome Westies, Nicci and Nelson,
and to Roquefort, who is quite as plump as Clover!
—N. C. W.

Watercolor and gouache paints were used for the full-color art.
The text type is Schneidler. Text copyright © 1994 by Mary Stolz.
Illustrations copyright © 1994 by N. Cameron Watson. All rights
reserved. No part of this book may be reproduced or utilized in
any form or by any means, electronic or mechanical, including
photocopying, recording, or by any information storage and
retrieval system, without permission in writing from the Publisher,
Greenwillow Books, a division of William Morrow & Company,
Inc., 1350 Avenue of the Americas, New York, NY 10019.
Printed in Hong Kong by South China Printing Company (1988) Ltd.
First Edition   10 9 8 7 6 5 4 3 2 1

Library of Congress Cataloging-in-Publication Data
Stolz, Mary (date)
The Weeds and the weather / by Mary Stolz;
pictures by N. Cameron Watson.
    p.   cm.
Summary: Mrs. Weed, a former teacher, and her dog and cat
enjoy their daily routine—with occasional disruptions—
throughout each season of the year.
ISBN 0-688-12289-2 (trade).   ISBN 0-688-12290-6 (lib. bdg.)
[1. Old age—Fiction. 2. Dogs—Fiction. 3. Cats—Fiction.]
I. Watson, N. Cameron (Nancy Cameron), ill.   II. Title.
PZ7.S875854We   1994   [E]—dc20
93-240   CIP   AC

For Mary Griffith, with love,
and for Ursula—again and again
—M. S.

For Bill,
with a special thanks to his mother
—N. C. W.

Contents

CHAPTER ONE

A Morning in Spring

M rs. Weed and Clover and Pocket live in a small house on a short street lined with trees.

They follow a peaceful routine. Rain day or sun day, blowy or snowy, seething or freezing, they do the same things every day at the same time.

They take their meals in the kitchen.
Mrs. Weed eats at the table.
Clover and Pocket eat on the floor.

Here is Mrs. Weed.

This is Clover Weed.   This is Pocket Weed.

Mrs. Weed is tall and skinny.
Clover is plump and proud.
Pocket is little and lighthearted.

Breakfast over, Mrs. Weed turns on the radio to hear the morning weather report.

Cloudy, with an 80 percent chance of rain today,
temperature in the forties.

Mrs. Weed looks out the window. The sun is up and shining. She opens the front door and steps out on the porch. The air is soft and warm and smells of lilacs.

"Well, they can't be right all the time," she says to Pocket. "Are you ready for our walk?"

Up he leaps with a *yik yik yik* of joy. He pulls his leash from the handle of the closet door and carries it across the room to Mrs. Weed.

His tail wags like a windmill.

Mrs. Weed buckles his harness, attaches the leash, and puts a plastic bag and a little trowel in her satchel, for tidying up after him.

Off they go.

Clover, an indoor cat, sits on the windowsill.

She watches as Mrs. Weed, taking short steps, and Pocket, sparking like a little rocket, disappear down the short street and around the corner.

Clover closes her eyes.

Little nap.

In exactly half an hour she wakes and walks to the door to greet Mrs. Weed and Pocket upon their return.

Now comes the exciting part of the day.

While Mrs. Weed does the housework (wash the dishes, dust the tables, count the dish towels), her friends rush from room to room, leaping over each other, dashing around chairs, through doorways, upstairs and downstairs.

Then they lie down, panting.

They are waiting for it to be lunchtime.

So the forenoon passes day after day.

But no!

Listen to this!

Rumpusing is taking place outside!

There are footsteps on their porch!

There is banging on their door!

! ! ! ! ! ! !

Pocket and Clover rush to the window seat and peek out.

Mrs. Weed whips her apron off and drops it on the sofa.

She changes her mind and hangs it on a chair.

She bundles it up and drops it on the stairs.

"Oh, dear," she says to Pocket and Clover. "The best thing to do is put it on again."

That's what she does.

Armed in her apron, she tiptoes to the door and peeks through the peeking hole.

There is a young man with a bouquet of flowers standing on the porch.

"Flowers for Mrs. Weed!" he shouts.

"Goodness, doesn't that sound funny," says Mrs. Weed, and opens the door. "It's my birthday," she says to the young man with the flowers. "I had quite forgotten."

She thanks him and carries the bouquet into the kitchen. She puts the slim, spicy spring flowers into a pitcher of water.

When she arrives in the living room, Clover and Pocket jump off the window seat and come to help look, and sniff.

Clover has a nibble of asparagus fern.

There is a card:

Love to Mrs. Weed, from a whole bunch of her grown-up third graders:

Paul
Peg
Bobbie
Betty Jo
Jill
Helen
Eliot
Matthew

Mrs. Weed smiles and says to Pocket and Clover, "I forgot my birthday, but I never forget I was a teacher. And just see! They do not forget either. I remember them, and they remember me."

But Mrs. Weed is not lonely, with her friends Clover and Pocket to keep her company.

"Now," she says, "let's forget all this excitement and be daily again."

Rain day or sun day, blowy or snowy, seething or freezing, Mrs. Weed and Clover and Pocket Weed prefer things to be the same today as yesterday and hope everything will be the same tomorrow.

CHAPTER TWO:

Noon of a Summer's Day

rs. Weed sits at the table, eating her lunch. She has a cup of tomato soup, a piece of toast, a cookie, and a glass of iced tea.

This is what she has for lunch every day.

In winter she takes her tea hot, in a china pot.

Pocket and Clover are on the floor, having their midday snack.

Pocket has two small dog biscuits.

Clover has two pieces of cat candy.

Mrs. Weed turns on the kitchen radio to hear the twelve o'clock weather report.

Fair and mild, temperature in the seventies,
no chance of precipitation.

Rain weaves in wide trickles down the windowpanes, tattoos on the roof, rattles in the downspouts.

Mrs. Weed opens the door and looks out.

Raindrops are bouncing off the sidewalks, sliding down tree trunks, dripping from awnings. A corner traffic light spreads puddles of color in the air—orange, red, green.

"As I so often say," Mrs. Weed says, "they can't be right all the time." She looks at Pocket. "I suppose you'll want to take your walk anyway?"

Pocket, tail wiggle-waggling, rushes to the closet door for his leash. Holding it in his mouth, he trots across the room and lays it at her feet.

"That's what I said I supposed," says Mrs. Weed. "I said I supposed that you would want to take your walk anyway. Let us get into our puddle-hopping outfits."

Mrs. Weed and Pocket each have a yellow poncho and an umbrella.

Pocket's umbrella is attached to his harness. Mrs. Weed carries hers over her head.

Off they go.

Clover, on the windowsill, watches them disappear behind a curtain of gray rain. She yawns a wide pink yawn, tucks her paws in, hums to herself, then closes her eyes.

Little nap.

When Mrs. Weed and Pocket return, he must be brushed with a towel.

Clover stays well away from him. She doesn't fancy wet fur, on herself or anyone else.

Later, when Pocket is good and dry, they have their racing game. Then all three go upstairs, planning to lie on the bed.

They like a snooze on a rainy afternoon.

But hark, hark!

Once again there is racketing and rumpusing outside!

Now there is scratching and scrabbling on the door!

It does not sound like flowers.

! ! ! ! ! ! !

Pocket dashes around on his clattery toenails, yikking and yipping.

Clover goes under the sofa.

Mrs. Weed draws a deep breath, lifts her chin, straightens her shoulders, and marches to the door.

She peeks through the peeking hole.

There, staring straight into her eyes, are the eyes of the biggest dog she has ever seen!

He is banging on the door with a platter-sized paw.

He says, *"Woof!"*

He says it again!

His woof sounds like a cannon going off.

"Shoo!" says Mrs. Weed. "You've come to the wrong house! There's nobody here named Woof!"

Suddenly a man appears beside him.

"Down, Ben," he says. "Down! Stay!"

"He has the wrong house!" Mrs. Weed shouts through the peeking hole.

"So he has," says the man. "And so have I. Our apologies. We'll be going on. Come, Ben."

Off they go.

"You can stop barking now," Mrs. Weed says to Pocket. "And you can come out from under the sofa, Clover."

They start upstairs again and this time make it to the bedroom, where they all lie down.

"Goodness," Mrs. Weed says, yawning. "I am sure he is a fine dog, and he did have lovely eyes, but I hope he doesn't come calling again."

Little rainy afternoon snooze.

CHAPTER THREE:
An Evening in Autumn

rs. Weed and her friends have finished their supper. Now she turns on the kitchen radio for the six o'clock weather report.

Clear and mild, temperature in the high sixties.

"Wrong again," she says, looking out the window.

Branches along the treelined street are tossing and thrashing, throwing their leafage this way and that. A cowboy wind whoops and hollers, spurring leaves and litter along the sidewalks. It tosses awnings, hurls garbage-pail lids like Frisbees down the street.

Now it starts to throw furniture off the porches.

Mrs. Weed opens the front door and rushes out to rescue her wicker rocker before it gets run over.

The air is bleak and biting. It pinches her ears and nose. The wind pulls her hair from its pins and tries to snatch her breath away. She rushes in with the rocker, slams the door, and sits down, breathing hard.

"It is gusting a whirlwind out there," she tells Pocket, who pulls his leash from the doorknob and carries it to her, head high, tail wig-wagging merrily.

What does he care for wind or wet, warmth or cold, dark or light, day or night when walk time comes?

Walks are what matter to Pocket.

Also food.

Also Mrs. Weed and Clover.

Also fun.

He doesn't want one more than the other.

He wants everything he wants.

Off they go, Mrs. Weed almost running as the cowboy wind herds her down the street.

"Git along, little doggie," she says to Pocket.

He skips and hops and leaps.

He snaps at leaves and twigs.

He whirls about.

"What joy!" he seems to say. "What a great time to be out-of-doors!"

And, "Oh, my," Mrs. Weed is saying to herself. "I do wish he'd hurry, so we could go back and get inside."

From her place on the windowsill Clover watches as they go into the windy and gathering dark.

She seems to say, "They really are mad, the two of them."

She has a mind to a little snooze.

But!

Now what?

Here comes a tree crashing down on the porch!

! ! ! ! ! ! !

Clover leaps halfway across the room, as great branches with quaking leaves appear outside her window.

She hisses and spits; her back loops high; her tail stands up like a whisk broom.

She goes under the sofa, growling.

Pocket and Mrs. Weed, blown down the street, arrive at their small house to find a forest lying across the porch, blocking the way in.

"Goodness, goodness, goodness!" says Mrs. Weed, and she claps her hands to her face. "We'd need an ax!"

But Pocket races around the side of the house toward the kitchen, and Mrs. Weed, the wind still pushing her, follows after.

"Thanks be!" she says to Pocket. "I forgot to lock up to-day."

They dart in, and Mrs. Weed shuts and locks the door, against the wind, against the weather.

"Safe," she says, breathing hard. "I suppose Clover is under the sofa. Let's go tell her she can come out now."

The three stand looking at the forest outside the window.

"It was a good tree," says Mrs. Weed with a sigh. "And now . . . firewood."

They go upstairs to bed, and all night the cowboy wind whoops and hollers through the fallen branches.

CHAPTER FOUR:

A Winter's Night

he grandfather clock in the hall tells ten o'clock in a deep old voice.

Time for Pocket's last walk of the day.

Mrs. Weed turns off the program she has been watching on television and switches to the weather station.

A young lady explains what the elements are up to, here, there, and everywhere, on a map.

Finally she gets to the elements Mrs. Weed and Pocket and Clover are interested in—

The weather on the street where they live.

Local prediction is for snow, ending by morning.

Mrs. Weed goes to the window and looks out.

The sidewalks are whitened, and the trees have put on cotton sleeves.

The snow-clad street has wet, snailing trails left by the treads of tires on cars going past.

Lamplight in houses across the street glows through a lacy, blowing mantle.

The corner traffic light is a web changing blurrily from orange to red to green.

When Mrs. Weed opens the door, a flurry of flakes flutters in.

Pocket smells the frosty air, and *yik-yiks*, and spins around. He likes snow.

Likes to push his nose through it, stick his head up and snap at falling flakes.

Likes the cold touch of it on his face and feet.

"Well," says Mrs. Weed to her two friends, "this time they are right. They say it's going to snow, and it is snowing."

Pocket rushes to get his leash.

His toenails clatter as Mrs. Weed buttons on his sky blue woolen overcoat. It has a velvet collar and velvet piping and a little pocket piped with velvet.

That's because his name is Pocket.

He has a nice rough white coat of his own, but Mrs. Weed made this extra one for him to wear in the cold.

Off they go.

Clover, on the windowsill, watches as they disappear into a whitened, whirling world.

She puts her nose to the windowpane, pulls back, closes her eyes, tucks in her paws, and waits.

When the walkers return, they all go to the kitchen for their bedtime snack.

Mrs. Weed has a cup of cocoa.

Pocket snaps up a biscuit.

Clover eats her piece of cat candy in dainty bites.

They go upstairs.

First Mrs. Weed.

Then Pocket.

Then Clover.

"Just think," says Mrs. Weed as they settle down. "Today the weather report was right, and nobody came knocking on the door with flowers, no big dog woofed for entrance, no tree came crashing down on the porch! A perfectly peaceful, daily day. Just the kind we like!"

They sleep together safely, and the snow falls softly, all through the night.